HELPING YOUR BRAND-NEW READER

Here's how to make first-time reading easy and fun:

- Read the introduction at the beginning of the book aloud. Look through the pictures together so that your child can see what happens in the story before reading the words.

- Read the first page to your child, placing your finger under each word.

- Let your child touch the words and read the rest of the story. Give him or her time to figure out each new word.

- If your child gets stuck on a word, you might say, *"Try something. Look at the picture. What would make sense?"*

- If your child is still stuck, supply the right word. This will allow him or her to continue to read and enjoy the story. You might say, *"Could this word be 'ball'?"*

- Always praise your child. Praise what he or she reads correctly, and praise good tries too.

- Give your child lots of chances to read the story again and again. The more your child reads, the more confident he or she will become.

- Have fun!

First edition 2001

Library of Congress Cataloging-in-Publication Data

Caple, Kathy.
Wow, it's Worm! / Kathy Caple. — 1st ed.
p. cm. — (Brand new readers)
Summary: Worm compares the appearance of his
animal friends to his own, builds a tower out of blocks,
tries to stay cool in the hot sun, and watches movies on television.
ISBN 0-7636-1152-2
[1. Worms — Fiction. 2. Animals — Fiction.] I. Title. II. Series.
PZ7.C17368 Wo 2001
[E] — dc21 00-041396

2 4 6 8 10 9 7 5 3 1

Printed in Hong Kong

This book was typeset in Letraset Arta.
The illustrations were done in watercolor and pen.

Candlewick Press
2067 Massachusetts Avenue
Cambridge, Massachusetts 02140

WOW, IT'S WORM!

CANDLEWICK PRESS
CAMBRIDGE, MASSACHUSETTS

WRITTEN AND ILLUSTRATED BY **Kathy Caple**

Contents

JUST RIGHT

Introduction

This story is called *Just Right*.
It's about what Worm says when he
sees Frog's big feet, Turtle's green shell,
Rat's long tail — and then sees Worm!

Worm looks at Frog's feet.

"Too big," says Worm.

Worm looks at Turtle's shell.

"Too green," says Worm.

Worm looks at Rat's tail.

"Too long," says Worm.

Worm looks at Worm.

"Just right," says Worm.

WORM WATCHES

Introduction

This story is called *Worm Watches*. It's about what Worm does when he watches different kinds of movies.

Worm watches a movie with clowns.

Worm laughs.

Worm watches a movie with monsters.

Worm hides.

Worm watches a movie with crying.

Worm cries.

Worm watches a movie with kissing.

Worm falls asleep.

WORM IS HOT

Introduction

This story is called *Worm Is Hot*.
It's about how Worm is hot and what happens when he tries to cool down by getting a fan, then another, then another, and then ANOTHER fan.

Worm is hot.

Worm gets a fan.

Worm is still hot.

Worm gets another fan.

Worm is still hot.

Worm gets another fan.

Worm gets ANOTHER fan.

Worm blows away.

WORM BUILDS

Introduction

This story is called *Worm Builds*.
It's about how Worm tries to build a
tower, but Frog and Turtle and Rat always
knock it down. Then Worm uses glue.

Worm builds a tower.

Frog knocks it down.

Worm builds a tower.

Turtle knocks it down.

Worm builds a tower.

Rat knocks it down.

Worm uses glue.

Worm's tower stays up.